FIRE FINCH

# WHEN TOMORROW CALLS

## • *SERIES* •

1. Why You Were Taken (2015)

2. How We Found You (2017)

3. What Have We Done (2017)

## ALSO BY JT LAWRENCE

The Memory of Water (2011)

Sticky Fingers (2016)

The Underachieving Ovary (2016)

Grey Magic (2016)

# THE
# STEPFORD
# FLORIST

JT LAWRENCE

FIRE FINCH
www.firefinchpress.com

*The Stepford Florist* is a work of fiction.

Names, characters, places and incidents are the product of the author's imagination or are used fictitiously. Any resemblance to actual persons, living or dead, events, or locales is entirely coincidental.

2017 Paperback edition

ISBN-13: 978-0-9947234-3-7

1st Edition

Copyright © 2017 JT LAWRENCE

Published in South Africa by Fire Finch Press, an imprint of Pulp Books.

www.jt-lawrence.com

Stock images by Shutterstock and Freepik.

Set in Bell MT

## DEDICATION

This book is dedicated to rebels everywhere.
Long may you make your own rules.

# THE STEPFORD FLORIST

# BOOTLEG VAMPIRE FACELIFT

**1**

Jasmine loads up the syringe with her client's platelet-rich plasma, fresh from the blood-spinning machine. She's just recently bought the secondhand centrifuge from the darkweb marXet, an absolute treasure trove of grey label bioware. She attaches a needle, holds the syringe up to the light, and flicks it with her violet nails. It isn't strictly necessary, but she's seen enough medical dramas on BingeStream to know how to act the part.

Jasmine pulls on some perfumed rubbersap gloves—clients prefer the vanilla-scented ones, while her tastes run a bit darker—and pumps the chair pedal with her open-laced KoBolt runners. She would have preferred a pair of Neo-Victorian ankle boots to go with the rest of her look: 50s Beehive Babette with a steampunk twist, but performing these vampire facelifts are murder on her feet.

She turns on her brightest smile and blinks her false lashes at Ms Fontaine. "Ready?"

Her caravan—as modded out as it is—isn't the ideal set-up for backstreet cosmetic treatments. Jasmine overhauled it with other intentions in mind. Still, she's not complaining. It's serving its purpose for now. She paints some local anaesthetic onto Ms Fontaine's cheeks and forehead, and the woman flinches.

"Cold," she says.

"Yes," says Jasmine. "It'll only take a few seconds to work."

She picks up her capped scalpel and uses the back of the implement to poke the skin stretching over Ms Fontaine's cheekbones.

"Can you feel that?"

The woman shakes her head. "No."

Jasmine inserts the needle into the dermis right below her client's wide open eye and injects a small amount of the plasma. Before she retracts it, there's a crashing at the door. Ms Fontaine bolts upright and Jasmine's needle misses puncturing her eyeball by a hint of a millimetre.

"Fuck!" Jasmine shouts, cool exterior shattered by the fright adrenaline. Her heart is a jack rabbit. She whirls around to face the three cops dressed in kevlar vests who have just smashed their way into the cabin. Ms Fontaine shoots up from the chair and puts her hands up.

"Don't touch her," Jasmine says, about to demand a warrant.

"We're not here for her," says the cop with the tranqtaser. His holobadge reads 'DETECTIVE SOLARIS', but Jasmine knows that already. His hand, holding the weapon, isn't shaking, not even a little bit. His bulletproof torso is of superhero chest-to-hip ratio. The other two policetrons look around at the bespoke steampunk interior with confusion and distaste.

"Don't touch that," Jasmine says to the cop about to touch her transparent timber cuckoo clock, but he does, anyway, and the clock sounds 'cuckoo!' and a copper bird shoots out and pecks his eye. He exclaims and drops his weapon as his hands fly up to his face. Ms Fontaine wraps her fingers around her throat and screams as if she's in a Hitchcock film.

Jasmine pulls the injured cop's hands away from his face to inspect the damage. A small cut on his left eyelid.

"It's just a flesh wound." Jasmine feels no guilt. He should have listened to her.

"You should have listened to me," she says.

Sometimes people don't pay attention to her. Perhaps it's because she's petite and wears fabulous lipstick. Maybe they assume because she's well made up, that there's no brain under the beehive. They assume incorrectly.

"Jesus Christ," says Detective Solaris, looking at her copper bolted walls and recogged microwave. "You've been hard at work. Is this whole place booby-trapped?"

"Maybe," says Jasmine. "So my original advice stands."

The third cop is tending to the bleeding one. She breathes right into his face as she tenderly wicks away the blood with a pocket-warmed wipe.

*They're shagging*, thinks Jasmine. She watches the way the woman's brow is furrowed with concern, and the way her backbone arches when she's in close contact with the man.

*Definitely shagging.*

"What are you doing here?" she asks Solaris.

Since blunt became legal, he'd stopped visiting her. She kind of misses him; a part of him, anyway. A very specific part of him. She puts her hands on her hips. "And why did you bring your minions?"

Solaris clears his throat. "Official police business."

"Really," says Jasmine. It's not a question.

"Jasmine Reeves, you're under arrest," says the female cop. She flashes the warrant in the air between them, too fast to read.

"Under arrest? For what?"

"Do you have to ask?" she says. "We just caught you red-handed."

"Illegal cosmetic surgery," the bleeding cop says with a wounded expression, as if Jasmine has hurt his feelings by breaking the law.

"This isn't surgery. This is a plasma injection. What's a little spun blood between friends?"

"You're not licensed to perform these ... what do they call them again?"

The female cop clicks the silver handcuffs off her utility belt. "Bootleg vampire facelifts."

The cuffs lock around Jasmine's tattooed wrists with

a hard snap. Hard metal on soft inked skin: botanical prints swirling into clocks and flying inventions. Petals and rivets.

If she notices the spark plasters on Jasmine's fingers, she doesn't say anything.

"I'm sure I can come up with a license if you give me 24 hours," says Jasmine, batting her quantum eyelashes.

"Nice try," says the female cop. Perhaps she hasn't yet forgiven Jasmine for almost taking out her lover's eye.

"We could trade favours. You can look the other way until I get the cert and I'll give you a lightning facial."

"No thanks."

Scowling, she pushes Jasmine outside.

"What about an iris color pop? A collagen lip plump? You'd be amazed at the difference it can make."


They step down, out of the caravan and into the chaotic garden, leaving a nonplussed Ms Fontaine behind. The property size is substantial: a Greenside double-stand with no building on it. Jasmine's caravan is parked in the middle of a thriving, blooming, bedlam garden, with not a weed in sight. It's all green leaves and seed pods; Bokashi tea soil; hungry creepers, blushing rose tulips, and giant torch lilies like sticks on fire. Hundreds of species of genetically modified flowers in every stage of bloom. One of Jasmine's striped cyborbees buzzes past their faces. The scowling cop sneezes. "What is this place, anyway?"

Jasmine doesn't answer.

# BETTER THAN MAGIC

## 2

Detective Solaris taps on the bars of Jasmine's cell with his ID chip card. She stops her rhythmic finger-snapping and looks up at him.

"Hello, you traitorous bastard."

"Hello, you rabble-rousing minx." Solaris notices the handcuffs lying open on the floor. "Hey. How did you get out of those cuffs?"

Jasmine, feigning innocence, whistles a tune. One of the reasons she wears her hair in a beehive is because she loves 50s fashion. The other reason is that it can hide a host of tools, especially if they're steampunk-inspired. Her high-spec steel hairpins can be used as thumbtacks, nails, and in a pinch: weapons, if held between her fingers in a fist. They're also pretty handy for picking locks.

"Get your stuff. You're getting out."

"I was just getting settled in."

She's been enjoying the last few hours she's spent in jail. Unplugged and undisturbed, she'd been able to practice with her latest invention. Jasmine clicks her plastered fingers one last time and the spark appears again, like magic. Except it's better than magic: it's science.

"What the—"

"It's nothing." Jasmine hides her hand behind her back and winks at him.

Solaris shakes his head and holds the card up to the lock. The mechanism springs apart and the door swings open.

She walks out of the cell. "Charges dropped?"

"No. Bail paid."

The detective opens a transparent evidence bag and hands Jasmine her Snakewatch back. She snaps it onto her wrist.

"What are you doing tonight?" Desire flashes in his eyes.

"Seriously?"

"Yes, seriously."

"You arrested me this morning and now you want a booty call?"

"Um."

"You're unbelievable." She'd take serious issue if he weren't so damn delicious-looking. The reality is she'd be totally up for a booty call from Solaris if she didn't already have plans for the night. It'll be good, anyway, to keep him waiting. Keep him wanting.

He sidles up to her, looks left and right to make sure no one sees him whisper in her ear. "I dream about the things I want to do to you."

She hands him off and walks towards the exit. "Tell that to your charge officer."


Jasmine skips out of the police station and makes her way towards the taxi rank. Solaris could at least have given her a lift home. She bumps Seth, and a little green bunny icon flashes when he responds.


Flowergrrl > Tx 4 rolling my bail. Life saver. IOU.


SD >> Hey?


Flowergrrl > Thanks for paying my bail.


SD >> I didn't pay your bail.

Flowergrrl > ??


SD >> Hang on. U need help?


Flowergrrl > No, all good. Catch u later.


Jasmine stands on the pavement for a minute, thinking, and a metallic navy blue limousine cruises past, then stops just ahead of her. The back door opens. Jasmine starts walking again.

"Ms Reeves?" says a sophisticated voice from inside.

She stops, looks inside. A mature woman in a black power suit smiles at her. Everything about her looks elegant. "Ms Reeves, may I have a word?"

"I don't think so." Jasmine keeps walking.

The limo drives next to her. "You're not interested in who posted your bail?"

Jasmine stops again, looks into the dim interior of the car.

"May we talk? Just for a minute," the woman says, tapping the seat across from her. "I have a business offer you may be interested in."

# A PRETTY ZOMBIE

**3**

"Why would you pay my bail?" Jasmine shifts uncomfortably on the expensive microsuede seat of the limousine. Her beehive almost touches the ceiling, and her rivet and blossom botanical print tattoos feel out of place in the champagne cabin.

"We'd like you to come and work for us."

"Us?"

"The Quantum group. Specifically, the Tabula Rasa clinic in Sandton."

Jasmine's heard of the Tabula Rasa. Latin for blank slate: as in, you walk in a normal human being and walk out shiny-skinned and brain-bleached. A pretty zombie.

Jasmine's snakewatch alerts her to a bump.

*Business card received,* it says. *Alexis Barnaby CEO Quantum Group.*

"Why me?"

"We need more therapists, and you need a job."

"How do you know that?"

"We make a point of scanning the profiles of potential employees."

"You stalked my data."

"You seem like just the type of person we need at Quantum."

Jasmine looks into Barnaby's clear grey eyes.

Thank the Net Jasmine makes a point of keeping her real details offline. Her online avatar is a total catfish. Only the paranoid survive.

"Ms Reeves. You're in debt. You're a paycheck away from being blacklisted."

Jasmine's watch vibrates again.

*Payment received from Quantum PTY LTD. 50,000 Blox.*

Barnaby smiles. "A week's wages in advance."

"That was presumptuous of you."

Barnaby laughs. "Most people would say 'thank you'."

"I'm not 'most people'."

"Oh, I know. That's why I like you."

"Look, I appreciate your interest, but I don't think I'm right for this position."

Barnaby stops smiling. "And where else are you going to get a job?"

If Jasmine really did need a job, it would be difficult to get one with her inked skin and extensive criminal record. Jesus, she detests living in a nanny state. Loves it and hates it at the same time, because if everyone else obeys the rules, those who don't are at a distinct advantage.

"It's not like you'll get a job as a SurroSis."

The SurroTribe is the last place Jasmine would get a job.

Without professional surrogates, the country's birth rate would be through the floor. Single fertile women who volunteer to assist infertile couples are afforded special treatment in almost every facet of their lives: free accommodation, travel, medical treatment. Each SurroSis has her own bodyguard and personal car. Fashion houses dress them, jewellers loan them compressed carbonites, brands virtually trip over themselves to place their products in their hands. They wear white robes and 'SS' badges in public so they can be easily identified and shown the proper respect: the opposite of a scarlet letter.

Solonne, the Matriarx, while outwardly chilled and bohemian looking, has a fierce moral imperative and a titanium spine. The SurroSisters, who live together in a gated community, have to be beyond reproach in every way or they are stripped of their pins. Solonne looks like a new-age hippie but she's marketing savvy enough to know how important brands are, and she won't stand for anyone tarnishing hers.

*Nope, no way I'd be getting in there any time soon,* thinks

Jasmine.

Barnaby sits forward. "We're on the other side of the line, you and I. We think boundaries are for … pushing."

Jasmine looks into her eyes again. Stainless steel irises return her gaze, then look her up and down. "Besides, I like your style."

Jasmine shakes her head. "There are plenty of cosmeticians that are way more qualified than I am."

"We're specifically looking for people who see the current laws for what they are."

"And that is?"

"Mutable."

"The law seemed pretty rigid this morning."

Barnaby smiles and blinks. "Well. You're out, aren't you?"

# HONEY LIGHT

**4**

Seth is waiting for her on the step of her caravan. It's quite a picture, him sitting there in a field of flowers, bathed in honey light.

"Aren't you a sight for sore eyes," Jasmine says.

"Right back at you." The tone of Seth's voice makes Jasmine think there might be sex on the cards, and that makes her feel slightly less exhausted. He stands up and moves out of the doorway, allowing her to step up and go inside. She almost trips over her grey cat, a British Shorthair called Chairman Miaow, who is shaking his tail at her for being late.

"Hello, Miaow," says Seth. "I  have a new collar for you."

"You bought my cat a collar? I think our relationship just leveled up."

"No. It was here when I arrived. Wrapped in a ribbon."

"Weird," says Jasmine.

"From one of your many admirers, I'm sure." Seth takes off the cat's shabby old collar and replaces it with the beautiful new one; blue suede with silver eyelets. "Now I'm wishing I'd thought of it first."

"Ha."

"But … I do have something for you." He pulls a small round tin out of his pocket.

"Ah, you're a gem. Thank you." She puts it on the counter next to an arrangement of charcoal magnolia-morph blooms.

Chairman Miaow pads over to his auto-feed contraption and presses the lever. It turns a cog which moves a belt, and the scoop is released, tipping a tablespoon of cat pellets into his copper bowl.

"I was worried," Seth says, watching Miaow munch away. "You disappeared off the radar after bumping me about bail."

He draws Jasmine towards him, and begins unbuttoning the back of her dress, nuzzling her shoulder.

"That escalated quickly," she says, half-joking, half floored by desire. The sensation of his lips on her skin sends a hot velvet current zipping through her.

"You're so goddamn beautiful."

"I don't want to hear that," she says.

"More importantly," he says, "You're a genius. And that's as sexy as fuck."

Jasmine lets her dress fall to the floor. Her nipples are hard against the synthsilk of her bra.

"Go on."

He kisses the inked lilies, the orchids, the falling petals of a plump black dahlia that turn into clock numerals on her pale skin.

"I don't know anyone as smart as you."

His grip is firm, and Jasmine's pelvis starts to throb.

"That kind of goes without saying."

He kisses her neck and the warmth flows through her, flushing her cheeks and dilating her pupils. His hand travels down her abdomen and slips under the elastic of her panties. He finds her bud and teases her in slow motion.

Jasmine luxuriates in his perfect touch, and lets out a long sigh.

Seth goes a little harder, a little faster. "If I could just have a fraction of your talent, I'd be happy."

"You're just as gifted as I am," says Jasmine, her body melting under him, her breathing becoming ragged. "And I for one am very grateful … to be on the receiving end of your talents."

Afterwards they lie, spent, on Jasmine's fold out bed.

"Thanks," she says.

"Oh, believe me, it was my pleasure," says Seth, trailing a finger along her tattooed back.

"I'm not talking about the sex," says Jasmine. "Although … it *was* pretty good."

"Only pretty good? My performance must be slipping."

"We both know that's not true."

He bites her shoulder.

"My god, you're delicious."

"I meant, thank you for tipping the cops off about me."

# EMERALD IRISES FLARE

**5**

Jasmine hops off the tuktuk at Tabula Rasa. A beautiful young woman with ebony skin and mirror braids is waiting for her on the steps.

"I'm Neo," she says, looking Jasmine up and down, hands hidden in the pockets of her white faux-snakeskin lab coat.

"Jasmine."

"I've been assigned to you," says Neo. She doesn't seem very happy about it.

"Sorry?"

"Teach you the ropes."

"Does Barnaby make a habit of collecting miscreants?" asks Jasmine.

Neo pulls her left sleeve down, covering the PLC barcode tattoo on her wrist. Jasmine would recognise a penal labour colony tattoo anywhere. Neo's still on some kind of probation, or she would have had that ink removed. Her mentor is obviously not a Surro candidate, either.

"I'm fresh from the slammer, too," says Jasmine. "What were you in for?"

Neo's emerald irises flare. "We don't discuss that here."

Neo leads Jasmine into the clinic building reception which is plush and crowded with large furniture, impractical cushions, magazine tiles, tiered trays of rainbow macarons and edi-glitter petit fours. A golden beacon of a carpet that makes jasmine think of the yellow brick road. Deep red orchid stems, roses and dahlias crowd a liquid mercury glass bowl. An antique silver bucket filled with real ice drips condensation onto its starched napkin. Two large glass bottles of Anahita water chill inside, and polished crystal champagne flutes wait on a tray nearby. Jasmine hasn't had anything to drink since before she was arrested. She plucks a cube of ice from the bucket as they walk past and pops it into her mouth. The receptionist clears his throat, making Jasmine jump.

"I didn't see you there," she mumbles past the ice-cube melting in her mouth.

The man purses his lips in disapproval. His glare is piercing; it's as if he can see that she has no place here.

"If you add a teaspoon of bleach to that bowl those flowers will last longer," says Jasmine.

Most people are oblivious to the myriad uses of sodium hypochlorite.

Jasmine's totally qualified to tend to the flowers in here. The client's faces: not so much.

Is an imposter still an imposter if she was invited to impose?

Once they reach the treatment wing, Neo and Jasmine peel off into a vacant room and Neo begins her orientation speech. No perfume, no piercings, no pinging. Flu vax stickers are mandatory, as are regular hand sprays and neutrabreath lozenges (they recommend *Bonbon Cinnamon*). No drugs or heavy make-up. Bright lipstick is fine. Wear your white coat at all times. Jasmine's invited to choose a coat of her choice from over a hundred different designs. All white, all calf-length, but each with individual bespoke details. Jasmine chooses one with a chrysanthemum illustration on the back, and Ming porcelain beads for buttons.

"You'll start with performing lightning facials and nano-lipo treatments," says Neo. "Once you're adept at sucking fat out of bored housewives' thighs we'll train you to do the more … complicated treatments."

# GOLD KIDNEYS AND A MELTED HEART

**6**

"Our most exclusive fat reduction treatment is the Gold NanoLipo Curve."

"That's a mouthful," says Jasmine.

"So, how it works is you inject the suspended gold nanoparticles into the fat cells, and then you use this laser," Neo shows her what looks like a smooth flashlight that pulses red, "to heat them up, and they melt the fat."

"Got it."

"So: anaesthetic sweep, inject, laser. You need to think like an artist and sculpt the shape. It's not just about weight loss. It's about creating the right curves."

"I can do that."

"It's also a good time to up-sell. A full body Swedish, a citric acid exfoliation. If they're willing to pay for the Gold Curve then chances are they have pretty deep pockets. Hell, if they're clients here then they've obviously got money to burn. Also, sign them up for a maintenance program. That way you score extra commission and make them feel you care about them at the same time. Two birds, one stone."

"Okay. Maintenance program. Got it."

"Good, because your ten hundred has arrived. You can collect her from reception."

"Already?"

"What? You need a toilet break?"

"No, I just ..."

"Barnaby told me you're an extremely competent and experienced therapist."

"Um. She may have overstated that."

In truth Jasmine had only had three clients, nabbed from her classified ad on the MarXet. She'd laser-targeted them by selecting extreme couponers interested in cosmetic surgery and then lured them with bargain basement prices and a fake professional profile on CorpLink.

"I'm only kidding," Neo says, without smiling. "You're a bright green intern. You're practically fucking glowing. Do you really think we'd let you near clients   on your first day?"

"Oh thank the Net," says Jasmine, hand on her chest.

"You could kill someone, you know. By injecting the wrong amount of gold, or by injecting it into the wrong place."

Jasmine imagines organs filled with gold. Gold kidneys and a melted heart.

"You'll be my shadow until I'm certain you're capable." Neo gestures that Jasmine follow her to reception. "Well, come on. What are you waiting for?"

Jasmine watches as Neo injects and lasers, injects and lasers, as if she really is a sculptor. The treatment takes ninety minutes, then the client agrees to a dermapeel and microblading. Jasmine is dispatched to gather the materials needed from the supply room.

"I don't have supply room privileges yet," she says, so Neo hands over her lanyard with her DNA chipcard. Before Jasmine leaves, she tidies away the used implements and picks up Neo's empty Tethys water bottle, gesturing that she'll throw it in the recyc for her. She walks towards the back of the building, passing treatment rooms, the sauna, the steam room, and the Lixair chamber. She uses Neo's card to open the supply room door.

It's a large space, packed floor to ceiling with smart glass boxes. She picks up the small steel shopping basket and clears her throat.

"Carbolix Mandarin Skin Peel," she says, and a container on her right flashes with a green light. She opens the box and retrieves the kit, placing it in her basket. When she snaps the lid back onto the smart box, it beeps red: *low stock, replacements ordered.*

"Soothe It Gel Silk." This time she has to climb a ladder to reach the top row on her left.

"Magnesium Mask."

While she's collecting the last of the supplies from the lowest row at the back, Jasmine catches sight of the securolock fridges.

Brushed metal, no handles, with a *Caution!* decal on the front, branded with a large red and white biohazard symbol. Nothing excites Jasmine more than a bold warning sticker. It's exactly what she's been looking for.

She knows better than to just try to wrench open the door. It would in all probability be booby-trapped with some kind of silent alarm and she'd be nabbed immediately, or worse. Instead, she takes Seth's small round tin out of her pocket and pulls the silicone clay out of it, then holds up Neo's empty water bottle and searches the surface for the best fingerprint she can find. She lifts it with the clay, then holds the newly molded silicone thumb along with the chipcard up to the bioprint scanner. There's a soft hiss as the suction is released, and the door pops open.

*Yes.*

While she's at it, she uses her—technically illegal—Klone app to copy the chipcard's DNA onto her snakewatch. She's sure it'll come in handy. Jasmine scans the rows of chilled vials as quickly as she can. Neo will be missing her soon.

VitaMAX. Colostrum Concentrate. Dermazip. eLixpray.

And then she sees it. SkinneRenew Serum. There are only three vials of it. If she steals one it won't go unnoticed. They'll know she was in here and realise she's the one who took it. But she won't have this opportunity again, so she reaches out and takes one, and slips it quickly into her pocket.

Her heart is thudding hard, and white noise rustles in her ears.

*You'd think you'd get used to this kind of thing,* she thinks, but it doesn't slow the hammering in her chest.

Jasmine closes the fridge door, careful to use the fabric of her coat as a glove. The fridge beeps red: *low stock, replacements ordered.*

*Shit,* she thinks, and then changes her mind. If more stock has been ordered it means she'll get to find out who their supplier is. Jasmine picks up the small silver basket and leaves the room. As she hurries she almost runs smack into Neo.

"Oh!" she says, trying to look less flustered.

"Cool it, newbie," says Neo, frowning. "What took you so long?"

Jasmine can feel the prickle of perspiration on her face.

"I—"

"Never mind," says Neo, grabbing the basket from her. "Just hurry up. Mrs Mantashe is ready to be peeled."

# LOCKER ROOM RUMOUR

7

"Darling," Jasmine says into her watch.

"Jassy!" says Keke. "How the hell are you?"

"I've had a good week so far."

"Spill!"

"I was arrested."

"Shut the front door! Hang on, I'm going to pull over."

Jasmine hears Keke's motorbike slow down and come to a stop. She pictures her on the hot, shimmering tarmac, leaning on the sexy bike, speaking into her new inflatable helmet.

"Congratulations," says Keke, a little out of breath. "Was it your first time?"

"Hardly."

"You need bail? A lawyer? An intimate massage?"

"No, but I did think you'd be interested to know that your locker-room rumour proved to be true."

"You didn't!" shouts Keke. "You're crazy!"

Jasmine moves her watch away from her ear. Keke's never been good at volume control.

"Of course I did. You can't tell me that kind of story and expect me to NOT act on it."

"You little sneak. You're amazing. Tell me everything."

"Well, basically, your lead panned out."

"No way," says Keke.

"I did some bootlegs and got picked up, exactly like you said I would."

"The mo-fos hired you."

"Yes."

"So you're basically a biopunk truther who is posing as a florist who is posing as a cosmetician."

"Yip."

"Ha! That's fucking beautiful."

"What can I say? I'm a woman of much depth and many talents."

"Oh yes, you are. I'm just picturing you now …"

"Wait, are we having phone sex? I feel unprepared."

"I'm picturing you in your greenhouse, surrounded by your mad burgeoning garden, with all your steampunk tattoo goodness, your beehive, your steel heels. You're holding a dangerously sharp needle and syringe, ready to inject some poor vain vacuous client full of god knows what. Under your lab coat you're wearing that whale-bone corset that I like so much, and those tiny panties. The copper ones, with the rivet detail. And you've got your pale make-up on and your perfect teeth, and a wide blood-lipstick smile."

"Ja, that's pretty much what the situation is like right now. I may have reached my zenith. Could anyone aspire to more than this?"

"You're like a … what phrase am I looking for? You're like a Stepford Florist."

Jasmine laughs out loud.

"Except, instead of being a robot inside, your cogs are on the outside, on your skin. And inside, you're you. The real you."

"I like that. I think I'll use that as my next avatar."

"And now you're going to try find those vials I told you about. It won't be easy."

"I have one in my pocket."

"Liar!"

"I'm on my way to HQ to have it tested. I'll let you know."

"If you're going to give me the scoop, you need to let me know how I can help. I can't just have it dropping in my lap."

"It'll be dropping in your SkyBox. Is your link still the same?"

"It is," says Keke.

"And you don't know me, right?"

"Never heard of you. No idea where the leads came from. Nada, nowhere, no one."

"Totally anon."

"Of course! But let me help."

"If I need help, I'll call you."

"Call me anyway. I want to see you."

# POLLEN&PISTILS

**8**

When Jasmine reaches the florist façade at 19:40 it's still open. The signage is street art: 'Pollen&Pistils'. The ampersand is white and has a neon pink glow.

"You're working late," Jasmine says to the woman behind the counter, a young health-goth emo with a half-shaved head and sharp earrings.

"Our regular florist is busy with another job and our boss is a real slave driver," says Kale.

Jasmine laughs. "I'll be back at work before you know it, then you can go back to your life of frozen soyshakes and RPG."

The woman whispers: "Seriously, I haven't worked this hard since the Slimonade case. I didn't realise how much actual business Pollen did. I thought it was supposed to be a cover. People keep coming in and wanting to, like, actually *buy* things."

"It wouldn't work as a cover if we didn't have real customers."

"Argh."

"Plus, we need the money! Who do you think pays for that terrible coffee inside?"

"I don't know. I thought maybe you freegan it."

Jasmine blinks at her. "What?"

"You know, freeganism?"

"You mean dumpster diving outside supermarkets?" asks Jasmine.

"To put it bluntly, yes."

"Wait. You think I dumpster dive for expired coffee beans."

"That's what it tastes like."

"God, the youth of today," says Jasmine. "So bloody entitled."

"Aren't we, like, the same age?"

"That's not the point."

"What is, then, oh Wise One?"

"You don't know how lucky you are. You're young, you're woke, and you're surrounded by beautiful flowers."

Kale sneezes three times in a row. "Don't remind me."

Her sneezing reminds Jasmine to keep working on splicing the apple blossom pollen with the natural histamine-inhibiting stinging nettle to relieve the hay fever effects. If it works, she can roll it out to her cut flowers, and it would allow them to access a whole new market.

Kale's eyes are watering. "In fact, if you must know, I think it's pretty horrible to be surrounded by dying plants all day."

"They're not dying! They're fresh and beautiful!"

"They're dying. They've been cut off from their life source. It's all downhill for them now."

"Only *you* could find flowers depressing."

Kale shrugs and lifts her sap-stained apron over her head.

"Not so fast. I need you here for another half an hour."

"Argh. I have tix for *The DarkReiki*."

"Half an hour, Kale."

The young woman hesitates. Her hayfever tears have scored lines in the smudge on her cheekbones.

"I brought new stock with me. Some tulip-cross-ivy, in the tuktuk outside. Will you fetch them, please?"

Kale sighs and puts her apron back on. "All right."

"You'll be rewarded in goth heaven!" Jasmine yells after her, and without turning around, Kale flips her the middle finger.

Jasmine slips into the stock room, redolent of zinnias and anemones and flower food, and draws the curtain away to reveal the secret entrance to the Alba headquarters. She has to stand on her toes to get the retina scanner to unlock the door for her, and when it clicks open she steps into the brightly lit open plan offices. Despite the hour, there are at least five people grinding quietly at their desks.

"Hello bunnies!" she calls, and some of them—the ones without noise-cancelling headphones on—look up and wave at her.

"Hello, Boss," says Seth, standing up. "I was wondering when you'd get here."

"I meant to arrive sooner. They had me peeling a super-rich woman at the spa."

"Gross."

"I'm actually finding it quite therapeutic. No pun intended."

"And you got what you wanted?"

Jasmine lifts her 50s clutch and snaps it open to reveal the vial of serum. She smiles at Seth.

"I did."

"That must be a record."

Seth smells like vetiver and grapefruit, with a hint of gunflint. He also smells like sex. Jasmine can't wait to get him alone. "Well, let's not count our chickens. We need to test it first. I'll take it to the lab. You can wait for me in my office."

"How did you know?" asks Seth, when Jasmine returns.

"Know what?"

A painting of a man with carriage bolts for eyes reminds Seth of the art at TommyKnockers, his favourite underground kink-club, and he makes a mental note to visit again soon.

"How did you know they were up to something at Tabula Rasa?"

"I don't know anything yet."

"What made you suspect them?"

"I got a tip-off."

"From who?"

"That's none of your business, Seth Denicker."

"A lover?" he says, inching towards her. He takes her hand and kisses her spark plasters.

"Close the door," she says, her voice gruff. He does, then walks over to her and pushes her up against the desk.

Jasmine's body relaxes in his grip. "Would it bother you?"

"Your other lovers?" he says. "No. I quite like the idea."

"Hmm," says Jasmine. "Not jealous?"

Seth thinks of the blonde Pharmax intern he had uninspiring sex with in the boardroom earlier.

"The only thing I'm jealous of is the fact that your lovers seem to be great informants. I seem to lack that calibre. Or maybe it's you. Maybe you know just how to mine people for all they're worth."

"It does take some practice," she says, lifting his shirt and inhaling the warmth of his skin. She bites his chest, and he feels himself grow hard against her.

There's a knock at the door, and they move reluctantly away from each other. Seth clears his throat, adjusts himself, and takes a seat. Jasmine smoothes her beehive, pushing in the errant hairpins, and checks her lipstick on the selfie function of her snakewatch.

"Come in," she calls.

The Lab Man is a nervous, wiry man with a moustache that jumps when he talks. "Got them," he says, "Got them!" and wipes his hands on his pants.

Jasmine crosses her arms and waits for him to elaborate.

"It's exactly what you thought it was," he says, then puts his index finger to his mouth.

Jasmine smiles. "Excellent."

"Fill a brother in," says Seth.

"My ... *informant* ..." she winks at Seth, "told me she'd heard rumours of Tabula Rasa injecting stem cells into their clients' faces."

"Um, that's gross? But not illegal. Remember the Lonehill story? They didn't even get charged."

The Lab Man goes white. "I don't want to know."

"There was a dodgy Thai manipedi place in Lonehill performing stem-cell facelifts in the back room. But these were manicurists and masseuses, right? No knowledge of chemistry."

"Seriously, I don't want to know," says the Lab Man. "I'm quite squeamish."

"So they ended up mixing stem cells and calcium in the clients' eye sockets, which, over time—"

"Argh!" exclaims the man.

"Cut it out," says Jasmine. "He'll faint."

Seth shrugs. "All right. I won't say any more."

The Lab Man's face looks like a wheel of camembert, and his upper lip is beaded with sweat. "Well, you can't just stop in the middle of a story."

Seth hesitates, then continues. "They basically grew these sharp bone shards in their eye sockets that were stabbing their eyeballs every time they blinked."

"Seth!"

"What? He asked me to finish the story!"

"You shouldn't take such pleasure in other peoples' misfortunes."

"I can't help it. I'm a terrible person."

"I won't argue with that."

"I just can't stand the stupid. So much stupid. It brings out every shade of my *schadenfreude*."

Jasmine taps her foot. "Can we please get back to the project at hand?"

"Yes!" says the Lab Man. "Stem cell treatment is not illegal, but stem cell *trade* is. 99% of all bio materials are bought with untraceable blox on the bioware marXet."

"So you want to nail Tabula for buying stem cells illegally?"

"No. I don't have a problem with corps breaking bullshit laws. I hate living in a nanny state as  much as you do. But where are those cells are coming from?"

"Well, they're grey goods, no doubt, but—"

"I'll only find out if I go back and look around."

"There's no way they'll let you back in."

"A girl can try."

"Why go back? Just report the bastards. Let the pigs do the rest."

"If I expose them now," says Jasmine, "we'll only get *them*. But if I dig a little deeper, I'll be able to find out who's supplying them, and get them, too."

"It's too dangerous," says Seth. "They'll know you took the vial. You can't go back there."

"I have to, if I want the whole story."

# HOT POCKET

9

Seth's apartment couldn't be any more different to Jasmine's caravan. A new biomorphic building, cool with smoked emerald glass and metal; glittering charcoal porcelain tiles. Smog-eating exterior paint and a solar Cool Roof with water catchment tanks. It's the ultimate lock-up-and-go: wholescale security, self-regulating, pet-free. It's spacious, minimalist, neutral, and air conditioned, and there's not a plant in sight, unless you count the micro-herb pockets on the kitchen windowsill.

Not that Jasmine is looking at the kitchen windowsill. She's tearing Seth's clothes off in the entrance hall.

"Good evening, Seth," purrs the apartment voice. "Welcome home."

"Thank you, Sandy," says Seth, pressing Jasmine against

the wall and lifting her ruffle skirt. He kisses her hard on the mouth.

"Were you working late again today?" asks the voice. "You work too hard."

"Not now, Sandy."

"You need to take care of yourself."

Jasmine laughs. He hooks the lace of her panties with his thumbs and pulls them down, kneeling in front of her as he does so.

The apartment voice won't be deterred. "Have you eaten? Shall I warm up a hot pocket for you?"

Seth looks up at Jasmine and wiggles his eyebrows, and she laughs. Then he starts licking the inside of her thigh, and she stops laughing.

"Don't tease me." Her cheeks are flushed with desire. "I'm already hot from earlier. I need you inside me right now."

"Sandy," he says to the voice, "play my Neon Tetra playlist."

The music begins, and Seth turns Jasmine around and bends her over the longline couch, pushes the black-striped skirt up over the ripe peach of her ass. She's fully clothed apart from the panties around her ankles.

He nuzzles and bites the pale velvet and she gasps.

"Now?" he asks. The bass makes them both vibrate.

"Yes," Jasmine pulls him closer. "Right now."

Seth makes her wait.

He goes down again and teases her with his tongue, can feel how swollen she is. He's so hard he feels like he'll explode soon. He tries to think of unsexy things to slow himself down. He silently recites the Fibonacci sequence till he gets lost in her. Seeing Jasmine in this position, smelling her, tasting her … it all swirls together and makes the numbers evaporate. He finds her sweet spot, and moves his warm tongue in wide circles, and she groans. A spiral to oblivion. It's her low, rolling moan, the one he knows well. The one that means she's so close to coming that there's no going back; like thunder before the storm.

Seth stands up and pushes himself inside her, and her groan gets louder. He feels her muscles contract around him, and it knocks the air out of his lungs. Slowly he starts moving, but she's so swollen and he's so hard that he only manages to thrust a few times before everything drops away from him and it's just them, just their hot skin and the rest is a wide open black galaxy, and they both explode together.

Later they lie on Seth's padded cineroom floor binge-watching *Extreme Science* and eating protein pops. Seth's hand is warm on Jasmine's thigh. When the episode about Mars tourism comes to an end, she yawns, claps the screen off, and stretches.

"I need to get home," she says.

"You don't want to stay the night?"

"Ha."

"I'm being serious."

"I thought you didn't do sleepovers."

"I don't. Not usually. But I'll make an exception for you. I have pajamas for you to wear and everything."

"No you don't," says Jasmine.

"You're right, I don't. Who needs pajamas anyway?" He kisses her shoulder.

She kisses him back, then pulls away. "I can't see you for a while."

Seth runs his fingers over her ribs. "Are you breaking up with me?"

Jasmine laughs. "I haven't heard that phrase in years. Cute."

"I knew it could never last," he says, sighing. "You're perfect, and I'm ... not."

"It's got nothing to do with you. It's business."

"Yes, Boss."

"I've got a kicker of a new assignment for you. A place may be opening up at Fontus and we need to move fast."

Seth's ears prick up. "Fontus? You're kidding."

"It's going to be dangerous."

"You know I like the sound of that."

"I'm being serious. You'll need to be very careful."

"It turns out that I'm naturally paranoid. Perfect for the job."

Jasmine pulls her clothes back on, hunts for her snakewatch.

"I'll bump you the details anon as soon as the position becomes available, and then we'll need to move fast."

"I'll resign from Pharmax tomorrow."

He'll miss designing drugs, or, at least, he'll miss the perks of designing drugs, but a new job is exactly what he needs.

Jasmine's ready to leave. "What'll we do with all the Mexican Mint I've been growing for you?"

"I can think of a few ways to make use of that."

Seth pulls her towards him, kisses her lips.

"In the meantime, we shouldn't have any contact," says Jasmine. "It's a big corporation with eyes everywhere. If they realize we're connected you'll never get the job, especially with the new case open against me. They'll do some kind of survey of your data. Delete any link you have to me on all your devices. And don't contact me until you absolutely have to. We can't fuck this up. This is the big one."

Seth feels a spike of excitement in his stomach. This is exactly what he's been waiting for.

"Yes, Boss."

# TABULA RASA RATS

## 10

Jasmine walks into Tabula Rasa with her heart in her throat. She's sure they must have realized by now that a vial of SkinneRenew is missing and checked their security cams. She's sure that a security guard will be waiting for her at the entrance. She steps over the threshold and holds her breath.

"Hey," says a male voice, stopping her in her tracks.

*Shit!*

Should she try to explain? Make something up? Or should she run?

"Hey," she says, a deep blush painting her cheeks.

It's the receptionist. "I just wanted to say thanks for the fresh flower tip. It works really well."

As she continues into the building Jasmine prays under her breath to all the gods who will listen. She needs to be able to get to the delivery entrance without being stopped. The delivery van leaves the bay at 09:30 sharp, and it's already 09:28. She rushes along the passage scented with orange flower and sandalwood, and uses her watch and the silicone clay thumb to open the biometric back door. She makes it to the delivery bay without anyone getting in her way, and hides behind a mesh cage of silver canisters. It would have been easier to come in using the back entrance of the building if it weren't for the extra security posted there; men with automatic rifles stand guard, as if this building is a penal labour colony instead of a luxury high-tech spa. The plain delivery van is parked a little way away from Jasmine, but she won't be able to reach it without one of the guards seeing her.

The driver appears and greets the guards, then unplugs and unlocks the vehicle. He checks his tile and something he sees makes him frown. He talks into his cuff. Jasmine guesses that he's noticed and reported the missing stock. She doesn't have much time to do what she has to do and get out of here.

She'd known something was off when Neo had explained that the spa collected their stock from their various suppliers instead of having it drone-delivered. It struck her as odd at the time, but now she knows why. The kind of places they're getting the stem cells from aren't the kind of places that deliver. She needs to get to the van, but two armed men amble up and stand in her way.

The delivery bay is a small, dim, temperature-regulated warehouse. There's enough space for a few delivery vehicles, and two of the walls are lined with stock that has not yet been transferred inside. Jasmine looks around for some kind of distraction, and spots a box in the corner marked *flammable*. She crawls as quietly as she can towards it, then clicks her fingers. Nothing happens.

"Did you hear that?" the guard closest to her says.

*Shit.*

"What?" says the man next to him.

"I don't know. I thought I heard something."

"Wanna take a look?"

*Oh fuck.* Jasmine holds her breath.

The guard with good hearing looks right in her direction and thinks about it for a moment, sucking his teeth. "Nah."

"Probably those rats again," says the other guard, tickling his weapon. "I fucking hate those rats."

A shiver travels up Jasmine's spine. She looks at the floor around her. She must not scream if a rat runs towards her. She must not scream.

"Well, there are regular rats, and then there are Tabula Rasa rats. I don't know what they eat in here but, hell. I once saw one that looked like a bloody kangaroo."

"Tell me about it. They deserve their own fucking nature documentary."

The men find this hilarious. The driver throws his head back and chuckles.

Jasmine clicks her fingers again while the men are laughing, and a spark appears. Then again, and she has her flame. She holds it underneath the flammable box until she's sure it's caught alight, then crawls in the opposite direction. A thin plume of smoke rises from the box, and the card crackles as it burns.

"Hey," says the guard. "What the—?"

They both see the fire at the same time, and run towards it, yelling, with their hands on their guns as if shooting the box will stop it from exploding. The driver peels off to the side to grab the fire extinguisher from the wall. He pulls the pin out and starts dousing the flames with the sodium bicarb foam.

Jasmine sprints to the van and sticks her tracking pixel to the underside. When she's sure it's in place, she steals quietly through the back door. She bumps Keke the pixel code for the van and a message to check her SkyBox.

Mission accomplished. Now all she needs to do is get the hell out of this place. She smoothes her beehive and takes a few deep breaths while she looks in the mirror on the wall. Neo's face appears behind her.

"Jasmine," she says. "Barnaby would like a word."

# VAGABOND

**11**

Neo pushes Jasmine forward, and Jasmine resists.

"I can walk on my own!"

Barnaby stands in her office, looking out the window.

Neo propels Jasmine into the room. "I found her. The cheek of her, walking in here today."

Barnaby swings around and cuts her a look that could freeze embers. Her arms are crossed smartly in front of her. "You have a funny way of showing gratitude." Expensive perfume scents the air: smooth carnation, incense, and cinnamon.

"Excuse me?" says Jasmine. She'll play dumb as long as she can, but the blood pulsing in her head is not helping.

"What do you know?" Barnaby demands.

Jasmine blinks. "I don't know what you're talking about."

The woman motions for Jasmine's snakewatch. Neo takes it and gives it to Barnaby, who tries to check her bump history but the information has self-immolated. She throws it across the room in frustration. It smashes a framed certificate on the wall, breaking the glass.

"What are we going to do with her?" asks Neo.

"Shut up," says Barnaby. "I'm thinking."

"Worse case scenario, she's already told the authorities," says Neo.

"The authorities are not a problem."

Jasmine thinks of Detective Solaris and his notoriously greasy palm. And he still tried to hit her up. Bastard.

"Then, what?"

"If the public find out about the serum they'll burn our reputation to the ground."

"The influencers," says Neo, "and the press."

"We need to contain it. Contain *her*."

"But we can't do that indefinitely."

Barnaby shoots more ice torrents in Jasmine's direction. "Well, maybe she should have an unfortunate accident."

Neo frowns. Jasmine's not sure if it's because she thinks the action is too drastic, or if she's thinking of creative ways to shove

Jasmine off her mortal coil.

"Will anyone miss her?" asks Barnaby.

She has no way of letting Seth or Keke know she's in trouble.

"Not likely. No family. Just a couple of rag-tag friends who we can take care of. I mean, accidents do happen."

"This is why we choose our employees very carefully," says Barnaby. "Ex-crims, punks, loners. We can't have people asking questions if they disappear."

"Reeves fits all the criteria," says Neo. "I made sure of it. She was perfect for the job, until—"

"Until she started snooping around. Stupid girl," says Barnaby. "Do you know how hard I've worked to be where I am? Do you know how many sacrifices I've had to make? Of course you don't understand. What did I expect? You're too clever for your own good. You'll never amount to anything of value. You live like a gypsy. You're nothing but a vagabond."

*Wait, what?*

"You've been to my house?" asks Jasmine.

Neo snorts. "You call that a house?"

"Of course we have. Well, not personally, of course. We sent a microcam."

Jasmine remembers the beribboned blue suede cat collar that arrived for Chairman Miaow, pictures the small silver eyelets. Turns out it wasn't a gift from one of her admirers at all.

"We check the living conditions of every prospective employee. We're usually very ..." Barnaby side-eyes Neo. "... careful with who we hire."

"I'm sure you are," says Jasmine.

"What do you want me to do with her?"

"I don't know," Barnaby rubs her temples. "I don't know the extent of the damage yet, and I can't think when she's in here. Lock her in the CryoGenix chamber until we decide what to do."

# ARCTIC MIST

## 12

Neo unlocks the huge steel door of the cryo chamber and the door opens with a hiss. The guards stand back and allow the women access. Jasmine's about to start fighting when she feels something bite into her neck, and she sees the empty syringe in Neo's hand. White light starts foaming in Jasmine's head, stealing her consciousness. Her knees give in and Neo supports her body, carrying her over to an upright glass pod and strapping her in. The restraints are secure, but Jasmine can hardly feel them as her whole body fades into numbness. Neo closes the door of the thin glass capsule and leaves the room, and the door auto-locks behind her.

Jasmine is breathing hard. She sees her chest pumping up and down in panic, but can't feel it. She thinks she'll use up all the oxygen in the pod if she doesn't calm down. The drug is pulling her eyelids down, but she resists. She needs to get out of here, or she'll never wake up. She writhes, trying desperately to get her wrists out of the restraints, but she can't feel her skin. Is she even moving? It doesn't feel like it. Her mind is mist. It's difficult to hold on to any thoughts, but she forces herself to focus. *Out*, she says to herself, *out, out,* and she wriggles some more. It feels like a superhuman feat, keeping her eyes open, and struggling against the ties. Eventually the fabric on her left wrist gives way.

*Oh, thank the Net.*

With one hand free, it's easy to remove the other straps. The CryoPod was designed, after all, as a space for a voluntary treatment, not a prison. Once her body is unrestrained, Jasmine focuses on getting out of the capsule. She feels around for any kind of handle or catch but comes up empty-handed. The air feels thinner now, and her lungs are pumping with panic. She's going to have to smash the glass, which is more easily said than done, because she'd bet her bottom blox that it's superglass: impossibly thin, and almost impossible to break.

But she doesn't have to smash the whole panel to get out. All she needs is a small hole that her hand can fit through, to reach the control pad and release the door. She searches her beehive for one of her heavy-duty hairpins, finds one, and puts it between her teeth while she takes her steel-heeled pumps off. She finds the place she thinks is closest to the panel and starts hammering the nail into the glass. It slips away on the first few attempts, and Jasmine worries it will never work, but once it penetrates just a fraction it gains enough purchase and she starts to hammer as hard as she can. Twenty minutes later the nail has penetrated half a millimetre. Her half-numb limbs begin to droop and she's sure she won't have the strength to finish the job. The thought makes her drop the hairpin and melt down to the floor. There's not enough air in the pod. She's not strong enough. Her hands are aching; her face is wet with tears.

Jasmine takes a few deep breaths and gathers her wild,

desperate thoughts. She pictures her caravan, her beautiful wild flowers.

*No family,* Neo had said. *Just some rag-tag friends.*

*No one will miss her.*

She thinks of Chairman Miaow, and wonders who will take care of him if she dies in here. *Although, to be fair,* she thinks, *cats are pretty good at taking care of themselves. Plus, she did a really good job in building that bespoke cat-feeder.*

She thinks of Alba, and all the important work they do there.

She knows that no one is going to save her, that she'd better save herself.

Jasmine finds the hairpin on the ground and hauls herself up, breathes deeply, and starts hammering again. Almost immediately, the nail shoots through the last bit of resistance, and the glass panel is compromised. Now she drops the pin and takes her heel and whacks the same spot over and over, and a small puzzle piece of glass pops out.

"Yes!" she shouts out loud, then covers her mouth. *Yes.* She puts her shoe back on, holds onto the sides of the pod, and kicks the small hole as hard as she can. On the twelfth kick, another piece of glass gives way, and the hole is big enough for Jasmine to get her hand through. The glass slices her arm as she feels for the control panel. There are three buttons on it. One of them will be the release mechanism. The top one? Or the bottom one? Middle? Probably not. She wishes she had her snakewatch; she could use the Selfie app as a mirror. She'll just have to guess and hope for the best. She closes her eyes and presses the bottom one, and the glass capsule begins to wheeze. Jasmine's body is flung backwards, arms once again pinned at her sides, this time not by fabric but by an intense vacuum. She feels her cheeks flatten against her skull as if she's in a personal rocket g-force experiment. The vacuum takes all the air out of her already screaming lungs. The blood from her lacerated arm bleeds into the wall behind her like paint being blown with a straw, and she keeps bleeding until there's a giant red Rorschach pattern behind her. Her lungs are slowly being crushed. She can't think of anything but getting oxygen into her body. She gulps for air, but the vacuum steals it all away.

Then all of a sudden it switches off, and her body drops to the floor.

She hauls air into her chest in one long, noisy gasp.

*Holy shit*, she thinks, over and over. It's like being vacuum packed. What is this cryo chamber really for? They're legal, used for cryotherapy treatments, but Jasmine has a feeling this machine is used for other purposes.

She's scared, now, to press the next button, but what choice does she have? She sticks her hand out again and clicks the top one. Arctic mist begins streaming into the pod. It's biting, bone-chilling. It's going to freeze her alive.

# SPECIMEN #586

**13**

The cold air fills the pod like white smoke. Ice crystals form on the glass in front of her, on her eyebrows, her eyelashes. Jasmine is shivering. Her skin is blue. Even her eyeballs feel cold and tearless, as if they've been freeze-dried. Blindly she feels for the hole in the glass and thrusts her arm out once more. Fresh air, fresh cuts, but now the blood freezes as it appears. Finding the control panel, she pushes the middle button this time, and the door unclamps. Jasmine leans her body against it and it swings open, allowing her to tumble out, stiff-limbed and gasping, and she falls in a heap on the floor.

She shakes her fingers, punches her thighs, tries to get some circulation going, and as soon as she can stand, she closes the door of the capsule.

The cold air keeps pouring into the room through the broken

panel. The pod's temperature gauge is on its lowest setting, and by smashing a hole in the glass Jasmine is sure she's compromised the thermostat. It'll keep trying to freeze the inside of the capsule until this whole chamber is below zero degrees. Already there's a layer of chill on the ground: she can hardly see her feet and she can't stop shivering.

The heavy steel door they entered through is locked. Jasmine pounds on it with her cold fist.

"Help!" she yells. "It's freezing in here!"

Surely the guards will let her out?

"Let me out of here!"

Surely their plan is not really to kill her? But no one answers her calls for help.

Her breath spools out in long white plumes. The air is so cold it hurts her lungs; makes them feel hard, as if the air she's breathing in is freezing them from the inside. She pants into her hands, trying to get some kind of feeling of warmth, and then sees her spark plasters. She clicks her fingers, but there's no ignition. Her hands are clumsy with the cold. She clicks again and again, and finally she gets a spark, and then a flame. The golden blaze fills her with a dreamlike joy. Fire! But then the cold air extinguishes it.

A flame is not enough. She's going to have to find something to burn. The layer of white air is rising, and Jasmine's feet are numb as she stumbles around the chamber, looking for some kind of fuel. It's a stark, minimalist space with no furniture. She flails around, pressing the walls, hoping for some kind of hidden storage space, but there's nothing. Just some square fridge doors—morgue-like—which she's sure won't yield anything useful. The only fuel she'll find in there will be for her nightmares. But there's nothing else in the empty room, so, at a loss, she opens the first door, and slides the heavy drawer out. It sails out smoothly, and when Jasmine sees the contents she jumps back. Specimen #586, it says on the tag. A naked female teenager with a shaved head lies on her back, arms crossed elegantly over her chest, her face crusted over with ice. Jasmine steps forward and touches the girl's skin, then draws back immediately on contact. Frozen.

Jasmine opens another door, and then another, and they all contain frozen bodies. An old man with a silver beard,  an old woman with an expensive haircut, a young woman with a birthmark in the shape of Africa, and a laparotomy scar.

The clinic is freezing people. The ultimate in reverse-aging innovation. Part of their quest for immortality.

Jasmine can feel her limbs and thoughts slowing, like her brain is slurring. Hypothermia is starting to set in. She takes off her shoes again and jogs on the spot, trying to think, her frozen feet like blocks of lead. In agony and desperation she throws her head back, and she sees a white sensor on the ceiling.

# CHERRY SLUSH LAVA

## 14

The rapid of cold air flowing out of the capsule doesn't stop. Jasmine is too short to reach the smoke detector, and there's no furniture in the room. She'll have to make a ladder for herself.

In any other situation, the idea of hauling dead bodies around a room and piling them up to make a set of steps would horrify her, but there's no time for sentimentality now. She'll be joining them in their endless icy slumber if she doesn't work very quickly. She pulls the frozen corpses out one by one, rolling them out and letting them drop on the floor before dragging them to the center. They're way too heavy to lift, and her poor co-ordination makes her stumble as she works. The exercise helps to keep her core warm, but her extremities are flashing with cold pain. The ends of her fingers are freezing and burning at the same time. Vasoconstriction. Frostbite. She rubs them together every now and then to try to keep her blood flowing.

Eventually she's dragged every last cadaver out of the lockers and she begins shifting them into a mound. It doesn't get anywhere near as high as she'd like it to, but it'll have to do. She uses her hands and feet to climb up the unsteady stack of bodies, and balances precariously on top. She tries to click her fingers but they're so numb now, like blunt sticks. She blows into them again.

"Come on," she says. She's starting to feel confused, now. The cold is numbing her brain. She forces her shutting-down mind to focus, and tries to click again. One, two, three, she snaps, which makes her think of some kind of nightmare version of Dorothy and the Wizard of Oz, and the ruby slippers. She thinks of the emerald city, but instead of it being made out of beautiful green glass it's blue ice instead, and everyone is flash-frozen as if they've been put under a wicked witch's spell. Barnaby, the wicked witch of Tabula Rasa. She pictures the Emerald City people stuck for all eternity in everyday poses like hanging up the washing, eating an apple, having sex. Like Mount Vesuvius burying Pompeii. But that was cause by fire, not ice. Cherry Slush lava. Jesus, she's delirious. Where was she? Sex. Wicked witch. Magic. She looks down at her spark plasters. She clicks them again, and after the fourth click, the flame comes to life. Slowly, she lifts her hand up towards the ceiling, beneath the detector. It may not be close enough, but it's the closest she's going to get. Her arm is shaking with the effort and the cold.

"Come on," she urges. "Come on!"

The LED starts flashing, and an alarm screeches, and water begins raining down on her. It feels warm. It feels like a scalding shower, because her body is so close to freezing. She has the urge to take off her clothes and to burrow somewhere dark and warm.

The fire alarm disarms the lock on the main door, and Jasmine makes her way down the heap of frozen bodies, shuddering in wide tics. She falls just before she reaches the door and can't get up. She leopard-crawls for the last few meters and when she makes it out of the chamber she wants to laugh and cry but her body doesn't have an ounce of energy in it so instead she collapses, cheek to golden carpet, and passes out.

Jasmine doesn't know how long she'd been unconscious, but when she feels Keke slapping her face and rubbing some warmth into her arms, she comes to with a shock.

"Jassy! Wake up!"

Jasmine moans. *Keke?* she wants to say, but her lips don't seem to be working. She sees Keke's helmet lying on the floor next to her, and her leather jacket, and thinks how warm the jacket must feel. She wants Keke to tell her that it's all been a dream, but when she sees where she is, she wants to go back to sleep.

"Wake up, Jassy," says Keke. "Stay with me!"

Jasmine opens her eyes again.

"We need to get you to hospital."

*Oh no, we don't,* Jasmine wants to say. *I'm fine, now. Out of danger.* But not only does her mouth not form the words, her limbs won't move either.

# EPILOGUE

"You got her here just in time," a male voice is saying.

A slice of bright white ceiling assaults Jasmine's aching eyes. "They freeze-dried my eyeballs."

Keke turns towards her with a huge smile and lifts her hands in excitement. "She lives!"

The doctor excuses himself with a silent gesture; motioning that he'll be back soon. The room is crowded with every cross-species flower Jasmine grows.

"God, I'm happy to see you," Jasmine croaks.

"The feeling is mutual." Keke offers Jasmine some water. "For a while there I thought you were a gonner."

The water paints the inside of Jasmine's mouth with cool relief. "What happened?"

"What happened? You tell me. When I read the file you sent me I tried to call you and you didn't answer. Then that pixel tracking came in and I realized you must have gone back to the clinic to plant it, and I got worried."

"The pixel. Did you find out where they were getting the stem cells from?"

"Yebo. Solaris arrested the owners of three different backstreet IVF clinics this afternoon."

Jasmine's brain is scrambled. "Fertility clinics?"

"Tabula Rasa was buying discarded embryos from dodgy IVF clinics."

"Fuck!"

"Exactly. But they're all going down in a big way. Your exposé skills are on point. Without the proof of where they were getting the embryonic stem cells from, the cops would've just yawned and walked away."

Jasmine sighs.

"Can't I credit you in some way, in the story? It's gonna be huge. You deserve the props."

Jasmine sits up. "That's the *last* thing I want. It's imperative that you say it came from an anonymous source."

Keke laughs. "You drive a hard bargain! That means I'll have to take all the credit for myself."

"I'm being serious, Keke. There's an important new job opening that's come up for immediate fulfillment and one of my men is being stalked for the position. I've been trying to get into this corp since we started. We can't do anything to compromise the anonymity of Alba. Do you understand?"

Keke stops smiling. "Of course. I'd never want to do that."

"Besides, you deserve the story. You're the one who tipped me off in the first place."

"It was a just a locker-room rumour."

"Well," says Jasmine. "You keep telling me your locker-room gossip and I'll keep offering you first scoop. Deal?"

"Deal."

"Well, actually, I did hear something the other day. It seemed crazy, so I brushed it off, but then I heard it again from a completely different source, and—"

"Tell me!"

"No."

"What? What about our deal?"

"I'll tell you everything once you're well enough to leave the hospital."

"I can't wait that long!"

"Sorry. But I know you. You'd rip that IV out of your arm and go chasing these guys down if I told you now. You need to get better first."

"I feel fine!"

"You don't get it. The doctor's not even sure you're going to keep your *toes*."

"Rubbish," says Jasmine.

Keke pulls the crisp hospital sheet away from Jasmine's feet, revealing stiff, marbled toes.

"And I happen to be very fond of your toes," says Keke. "So get better, and then we'll talk."

Jasmine leans back again and sighs. "Okay."

"Also, I'm tired of cat-sitting. You need to get your ass home."

"What are you talking about? You don't even have to feed him. The machine does that."

"I know. But that cat makes me nervous."

"Chairman Miaow makes you nervous."

"It's not him, it's me. You know I'm not good at keeping things alive."

"That reminds me," says Jasmine. "What about the dead bodies?"

Keke does a double-take. "The what-what?"

"The frozen bodies. There were, like, two dozen corpses in that chamber with me."

Keke frowns. "There were no bodies, alive or dead. As soon as Barnaby realized how deep the shit was, she was off in her private Volanter. The rest of the staff scarpered, too. When I got there it was a fucking ghost town. The cops didn't find anyone, either."

"I know what I saw."

"Hallucinations are pretty normal for someone who was in your condition. You were hypothermic … I don't blame you for seeing dead people. It was pretty bad. The doc said you would have died if I hadn't shared my body heat with you."

"Now … that sounds interesting."

"Don't get any ideas, but I had to take your clothes off because they were wet."

"That's what she said."

Keke laughs. "It gets kinkier than that."

"I'm listening."

"I had to strap you to my back so that you wouldn't fall off."

"Fall off what?"

"The bike!"

"You strapped me onto your bike."

"It's the only way I could get you here fast enough. Lunch hour traffic in ChinaCity/Sandton. The struggle is real."

"You strapped me to your bike. Naked. Through rush hour traffic."

"What? We made headline news! Loads of taxi drivers hooted and waved us straight through."

Keke laughs at her own joke. "Oh, relax. I'm only kidding about the news part. And the naked part. I put my leather jacket over you."

"That was kind."

"Yes, well, I do like to take care of my sources." Keke puts a hand on Jasmine's knee.

"You can joke all you like. Those frozen bodies were real."

"Okay," says Keke, grabbing her helmet off the side table and inflating it. "I'll investigate."

"I think it must have had something to do with their Immortality Program. But who were the people? Volunteers? Victims? An inquisitive mind wants to know."

"You'll know as soon as I do."

"You're leaving? You didn't even bring me Get Better Soon snacks."

"I'll be back soon."

"Booty call?"

"DNA date."

Keke is the only person Jasmine knows who dates specifically to gather work contacts.

"Politician? CEO? Scientist?"

"Even better. He's a hacker with little regard for the law. And if he's as good as everyone says he is, then … let's just say he'll come in very handy."

"Then go forth and conquer," Jasmine closes her eyes, feels

the beginning of sleep pulling at her consciousness. "And when you get back, I want to know everything."

# WHEN TOMORROW CALLS

## • *SERIES* •

1. Why You Were Taken (2015)

2. How We Found You (2017)

3. What Have We Done (2017)

## ALSO BY JT LAWRENCE

The Memory of Water (2011)

Sticky Fingers (2016)

The Underachieving Ovary (2016)

Grey Magic (2016)

## ABOUT THE AUTHOR

JT Lawrence is an Amazon bestselling author, playwright & bookdealer. She lives in Parkview, Johannesburg, in a house with a red front door.

\* \* \*

## STAY IN TOUCH

Be notified of giveaways &
new releases by signing up for JT Lawrence's mailing list
via Facebook or at www.jt-lawrence.com